Message From the Author

Sign up at Gean's website at www.pgshriver.com to receive a free video reading of the first Texas Festivals picture book featuring myself and my puppet Sally! But, I'm only giving away a few of these video readings, so hurry before the downloads run out!

Master Stinky Dances

Gean Penny

For

MiMi's Stink-A-Roo

and

LogiBear, too

Thank you to all the kittens born in this world that provide companionship, entertainment, and cuddles to us two legged critters.

Crouch, step!
Pounce, pounce!
Leap, jump!
Crunch, crunch!

A cricket caught beneath tiny claws. Another chewed by tiny teeth.
"I am the mightiest hunter!" One kitten yowls as he traps his prey.

"I am the sneakiest hunter!"

Another kitten cries. He lowers his head to his paws and shakes his fluffy tail.

"I am the boldest hunter!" A strong kitten growls fearlessly into a bright light.

"I am the prettiest hunter!" A calico kitten purrs.

She sits up, licks her paw, and strokes her ear.

"I am the luckiest hunter!"

A tabby kitten grins. An extra large cricket dangles between his teeth.

"We are the best team of hunters!"

Twin kittens cry, a squirming bug caught beneath their four front paws.

"No! We are the best!"

More twins contest as a trapped cricket wiggles between them.

"I am the hungriest of hunters," a frail voice calls from the shadows.

"Who's that?" Two kittens mew looking up from their snack.

"Yes, who are you?" Two more growl between chews.

"I can't see you! Come into the light!" The boldest kitten arches his back, fluffs his tail, and hisses toward the voice.

"Yes, come! Yes, come!" The kittens sing. They crouch and stare into the darkness ready to pounce as one onto a larger prey.

"I am so hungry. I can hardly walk." Weakly, the strange creature parts the grass.

The kittens spy a pointy nose with long trembling whiskers. Next appears a fluffy body. Then the kittens' eyes pop with delight! The most beautiful tail they've ever seen sways behind the stranger!

"May I have a tiny bit of bug?" The feeble voice asks, but one selfish kitten protests standing tall and spreading his claws! "This is our farm! We hunt here! Go find another!"

"I've searched everywhere. I'm far from my home. I need only the smallest of meals, but none are found." The stranger's head droops. The tips of his teeny ears lower.

"Mama always says to share!" One twin reminds the others. His brother pounces and rolls him over replying, "Not with strangers, you dork!" The two kittens hiss, spit, and tumble into the darkness.

"Oh, my! You have the most beautiful tail I've ever seen!" Admires the pretty one. She walks slowly and carefully around the back of the strange creature for a closer look.

"Thank you!" The creature stands tall and proud. He gives his tail a little shake in her direction. The sudden motion causes her to hop backward.

"But your nose sure is pointy!" The lucky kitten calls as he sneaks over for a better look. "Did you get it caught in something?" He asks reaching a paw forward. He taps at the air above the long, striped snout.

"I was born with this nose." The creature looks over his long nose. Two large, green eyes peer back at him as whiskers wiggle.

"You have a wonderful coat!" Two other kittens sing out. "Almost as wonderful as ours!" They jump closer for a better look.

The strange animal turns quickly in the light to show off his fur. The glossy black shimmers and shines. "Thank you!" He turns proudly forgetting his hunger. He lifts his head and shakes his tail. The nine kittens pounce and play around him.

"And you do smell funny!" The mighty kitten sniffs the air. He backs and turns his face away from the smell.

"I do? I was born this way. All of my family was born this way." The creature lowers his head and remembers.

"Where is your family?" One kitten prowls slowly toward the stranger's sad face. She crouches low.

She feels his sadness. It reminds her of the time she lost a brother.

"My family is gone. Once there were many bugs to eat and many places to hunt. Now there are fewer trees and more two legged creatures with water that kills the bugs. Once I was a master of a large family. Now I am alone and hungry."

A tear drips off his long nose slowly, plopping on the dry ground before the crouched kitten. The kitten reaches forward and covers the wet spot with her paw. The creature's fluffy tail droops at the top and his long nose lowers to the ground.

"We have two legged creatures in the farmhouse!" The smallest kitten mews.

"A master! Ooh, how great that must be!" The pretty kitten calls from behind the stranger. "What is a master?" She wonders aloud reaching up to bat the tip of the stranger's tail. Her move frightens him, and his tail stiffens.

Pooooof! A light mist fills the air around her.

"A master is like Mr. Moe and Mr. Tom. I will be a master someday, too!" The bold kitten answers.

"Oh, I do not like Mr. Moe and Mr. Tom. They fight too much. They are mean!" The pretty kitten pouts. "One time, Mr. Moe scratched me here!" She sadly paws the top of her head.

"Eyuuuwwww! The Master stinks!" One kitten cries as the mist travels on the breeze.
"Master Stinky! Master Stinky!"
Eight kittens sing, running, jumping, and pouncing away.
They flip each other over trying to outrun the smell.

"I'm sorry. When I get scared, I... I... I poof." He moves quickly and gracefully turning in circles, this way and that way, one step left, two steps right. He speaks softly to the kittens to calm them. His tail sways, straight and tall, plumes fluttering in the night like down feathers.

"I don't think the smell is that bad. They're just mean!" The pretty kitten purrs. "The way you dance makes up for it, I think!" She smiles, facing him, moving to the right, then left in time with Master Stinky. Circling they step gracefully while the rest watch.

The mightiest kitten raises his paws scratching at air. "Well, you do have some moves, Master Stinky."

"Mother calls it grace! Grace, grace, grace!" All the kittens sing.

"You are a lovely dancer, Master Stinky!" The boldest kitten agrees. Skunk and kittens circle beneath the bright barnyard light. Forgotten bugs fall and chirp around them.

Master Stinky dances.

Crickets sing and frogs call lending their tune to the dance, a dance of friendship between ones so different.

Suddenly all falls quiet. The dance stops. Skunk and kittens freeze.

One tiny kitten approaches their new friend with lowered head. A large cricket dangles by one leg from the kitten's mouth. "I caught this for you, Master Stinky." The kitten quietly purrs.

"Thank you, friend!" The skunk bows his head. Master Stinky accepts the largest cricket he has ever seen from the tiniest kitten on the farm.

All the kittens cheer!

This tiny kitten is the runt of the litters, but he has the biggest heart of all. Though he is the last to hunt, he gives his first cricket to a new friend in need!

Reminder from the Author

Remember to sign up at Gean's website at www.pgshriver.com to receive a free audio reading of this book!

About the Author

Gean Penny has written several books for children, including three series. She lives on a small horse farm in Texas with her family, where they sometimes watch their barn kittens play beneath the security light. One night, while the kittens played, Gean watched a skunk wander into the light searching for bugs. That night became the inspiration for this book!

More Books by Gean Penny (aka PG Shriver)

The Stinker Books

Adventures of Runt and Arnold

Texas Festival Series

The Lonely Chair (An Amazon #1 Bestseller)

CPSIA information can be obtained
at www.ICGtesting.com
Printed in the USA
BVHW020337110720
583430BV00007B/37

* 9 7 8 1 9 5 2 7 2 6 2 1 7 *